WELCOME TO
PASSPORT TO READING
A beginning reader's ticket to a brand-new world!

Every book in this program is designed to build read-along and read-alone skills, level by level, through engaging and enriching stories. As the reader turns each page, he or she will become more confident with new vocabulary, sight words, and comprehension.

These PASSPORT TO READING levels will help you choose the perfect book for every reader.

READING TOGETHER
Read short words in simple sentence structures together to begin a reader's journey.

READING OUT LOUD
Encourage developing readers to sound out words in more complex stories with simple vocabulary.

READING INDEPENDENTLY
Newly independent readers gain confidence reading more complex sentences with higher word counts.

READY TO READ MORE
Readers prepare for chapter books with fewer illustrations and longer paragraphs.

This book features sight words from the educator-supported Dolch Sight Words List. This encourages the reader to recognize commonly used vocabulary words, increasing reading speed and fluency.

For more information, please visit passporttoreadingbooks.com.

Enjoy the journey!

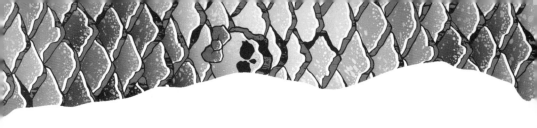

Little, Brown and Company

Hachette Book Group
1290 Avenue of the Americas, New York, NY 10104
Visit us at lb-kids.com

Little, Brown and Company is a division of Hachette Book Group, Inc. The Little, Brown name and logo are trademarks of Hachette Book Group, Inc.

The publisher is not responsible for websites (or their content) that are not owned by the publisher.

First Edition: April 2016

ISBN 978-0-316-30130-5

10 9 8 7 6 5 4 3 2 1

CW

Printed in the United States of America

Passport to Reading titles are leveled by independent reviewers applying the standards developed by Irene Fountas and Gay Su Pinnell in *Matching Books to Readers: Using Leveled Books in Guided Reading*, Heinemann, 1999.

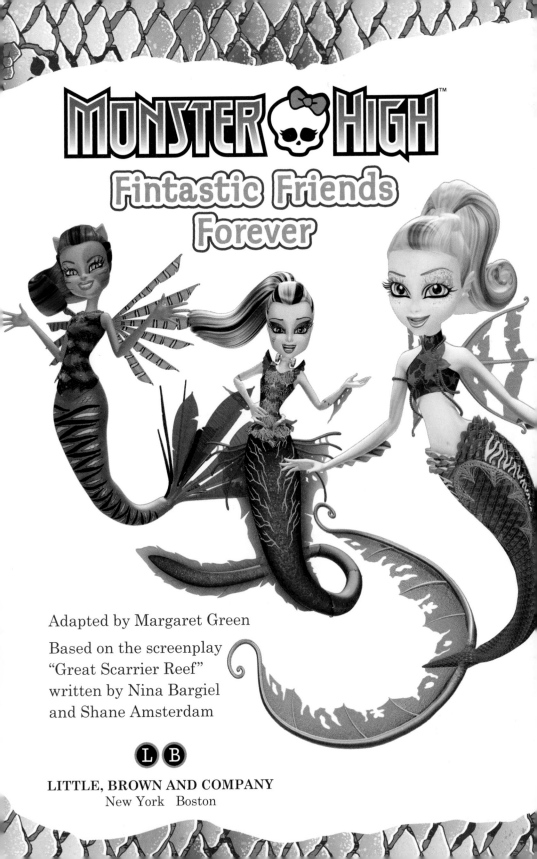

MONSTER HIGH™
Fintastic Friends Forever

Adapted by Margaret Green

Based on the screenplay
"Great Scarrier Reef"
written by Nina Bargiel
and Shane Amsterdam

L B

LITTLE, BROWN AND COMPANY
New York   Boston

Lagoona Blue loved Monster High, and she loved her Monster High ghoulfriends. The ghouls had a deep friendship. Then they realized that even old friendships can get deeper!

Frankie Stein, Draculaura,
and Clawdeen Wolf were
performing in a dance recital.
Toralei Stripe taught them some
crazy moves, but Lagoona still
cheered them on!

At the recital, Lagoona
was embarrassed onstage.
When a video of her embarrassing
moment went viral, the ghouls
broke the news to her gently.

Soon after, Lagoona and her friends
were sucked into a vortex at
the Monster High swimming pool.
It brought them to the
Great Scarrier Reef.

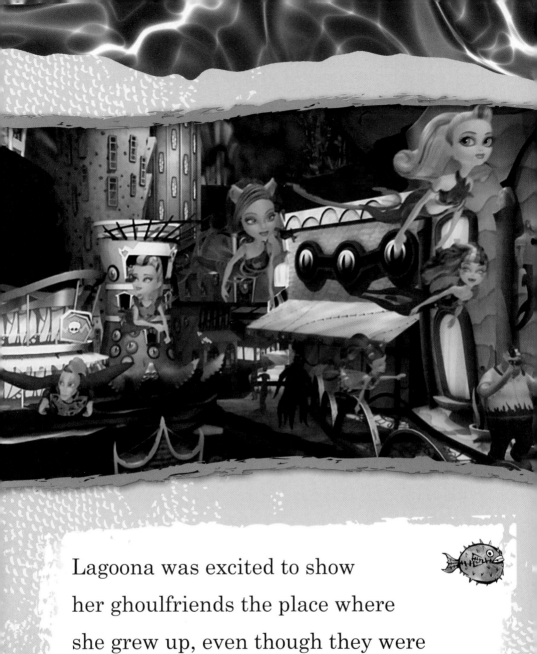

Lagoona was excited to show
her ghoulfriends the place where
she grew up, even though they were
trying to find a way back to Monster High.

They even got
to meet her family!
Lagoona's friends loved
her little sister, Kelpie.

And they were grateful
to Lagoona's dad for
warning them about
a giant sea monster
called the Kraken.

When Lagoona decided she
needed to face the Kraken
to confront her fears, her
ghoulfriends did what any
good friends would do: They
tried to persuade her not to!

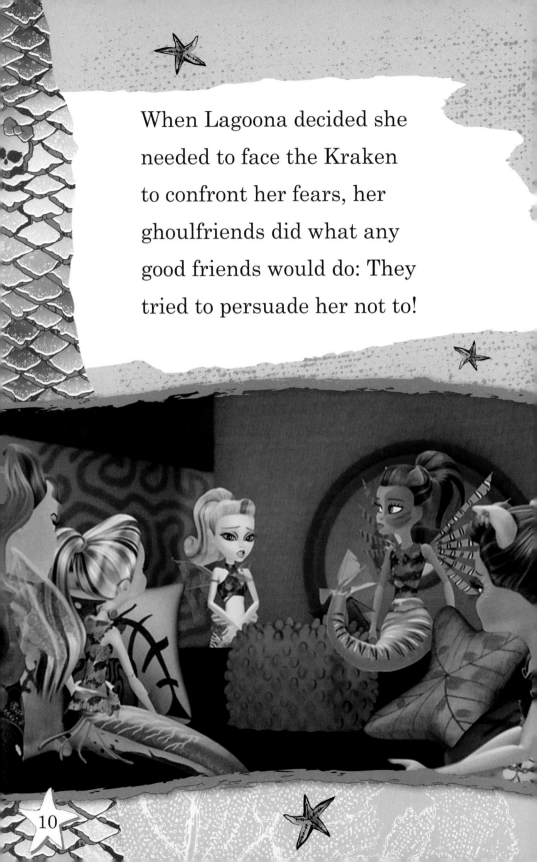

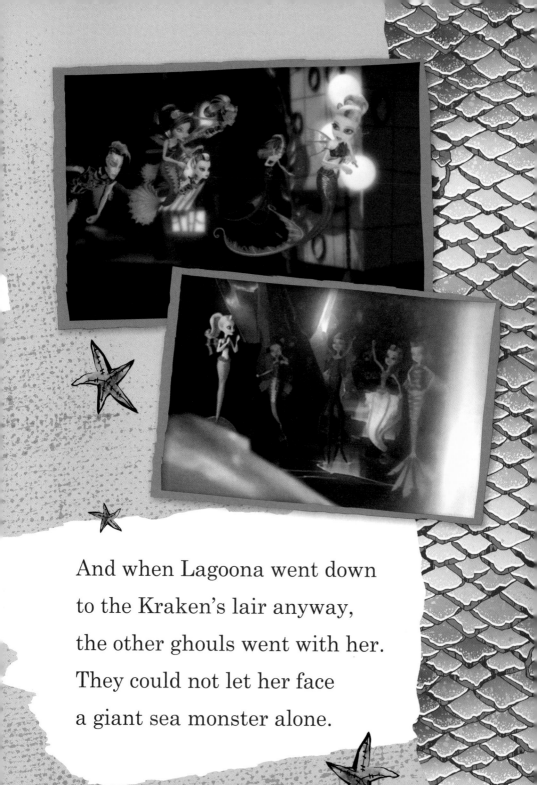

And when Lagoona went down
to the Kraken's lair anyway,
the other ghouls went with her.
They could not let her face
a giant sea monster alone.

With her friends by her side,
Lagoona faced the Kraken.
Then she had to face
an even bigger fear: being onstage.
She tried to dance, but she froze!
The other ghouls were there
to catch her.

Things got scarier when
the Kraken showed up.

Lagoona's friends helped her lead him
away from the Great Scarrier Reef.

The Kraken followed them
all the way back to Monster High!
Together, the ghouls came up with a plan
to stop him from destroying their school.
Lagoona knew that with ghoulfriends
like these, she could do anything.

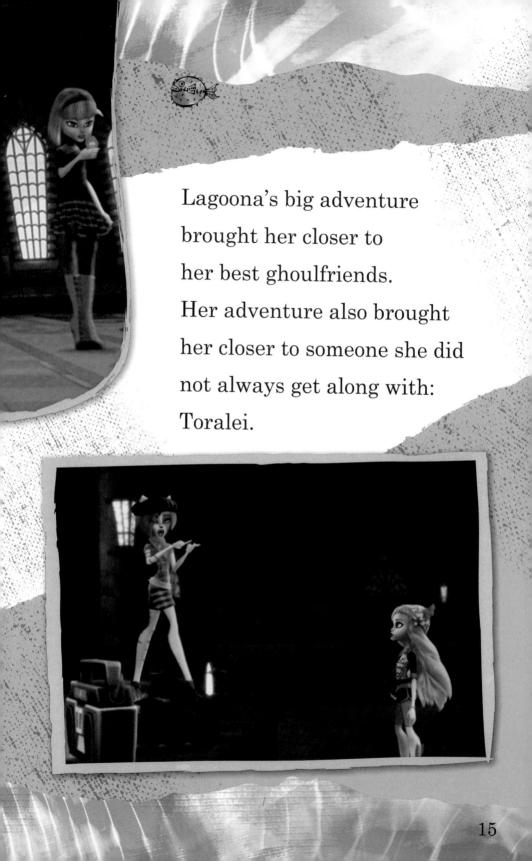

Lagoona's big adventure brought her closer to her best ghoulfriends. Her adventure also brought her closer to someone she did not always get along with: Toralei.

Toralei liked to play mean tricks
on Lagoona and the other ghouls.
She was the one who made Lagoona's
embarrassing moment go viral!

Lagoona decided she'd had enough.

She uninvited Toralei from
a big party that night.

When Toralei found out, she was fuming.

She and Lagoona had a huge fight.

But when Lagoona needed her,
Toralei proved to Lagoona
that she was a true friend.
She helped the ghouls come up
with a dance for the undersea
talent show.

And when Lagoona
froze onstage,
Toralei defended her.

She even used her crazy dance moves
to try to distract the Kraken
from destroying Monster High!

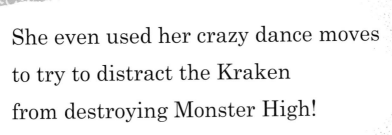

The next time Lagoona threw a party, she made sure that her ghoulfriend Toralei was invited.

Lagoona also reunited with
an old friend back in the
Great Scarrier Reef,
but it did not happen easily.
At first, Lagoona's old dance partner,
Kala Mer'ri, was really mean to her.

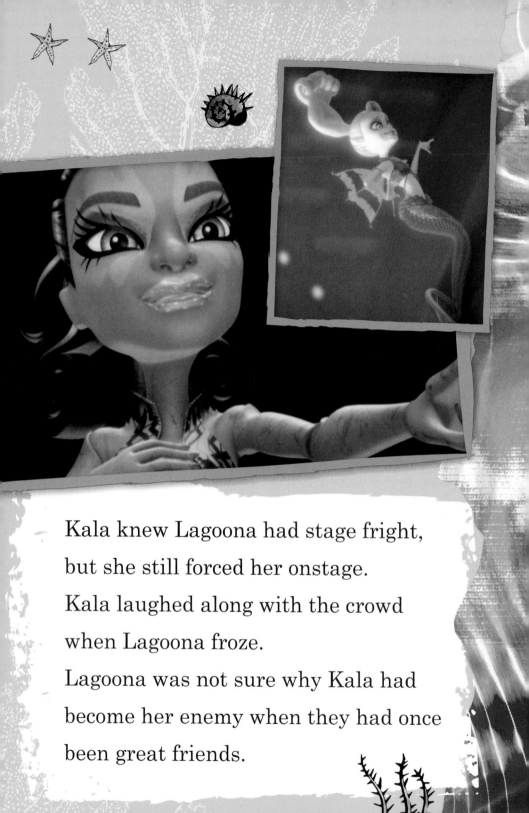

Kala knew Lagoona had stage fright, but she still forced her onstage. Kala laughed along with the crowd when Lagoona froze.

Lagoona was not sure why Kala had become her enemy when they had once been great friends.

All she knew was that a long time ago, she tried to comfort Kala by telling her friend that she would dance better than the old Kraken.

Then Kala had tied Lagoona's shoes together! That was the last time Lagoona took the stage.

But now she had to face her fear. So when Kala challenged her to enter the undersea talent show, Lagoona agreed.

Kala did everything she could
to upset Lagoona.

She and her friend Pearl Serpentine
tricked Lagoona into thinking
she needed to face the Kraken
to get rid of her stage fright.

Luckily, Lagoona had true ghoulfriends
who helped her survive that encounter.
Then Kala revealed that she had lied—
right before Lagoona had to go onstage!

But when Lagoona's ghoulfriends
helped her get the crowd on her side,
Kala summoned the Kraken
from the deep waters.
She brought him up to Monster High!

Lagoona wanted to find out
why Kala was doing this.
Her old friend said she was tired of
being made fun of for being different.
When Lagoona shared that being different
was a good thing at Monster High,
Kala called off the Kraken.

Then Kala introduced
the big sea monster as her dad!
Now Lagoona understood.

Everyone was afraid
of the Kraken,
so Kala was ashamed
to admit he was her father.

Lagoona told Kala she was sorry
she had misjudged the Kraken.
Then she invited her old friend
to join her at Monster High.

Lagoona Blue loved having
so many freaky-cool ghoulfriends.
And after her big adventure
in the Great Scarrier Reef,
she had even more ghouls
to call friends!